Cinderella

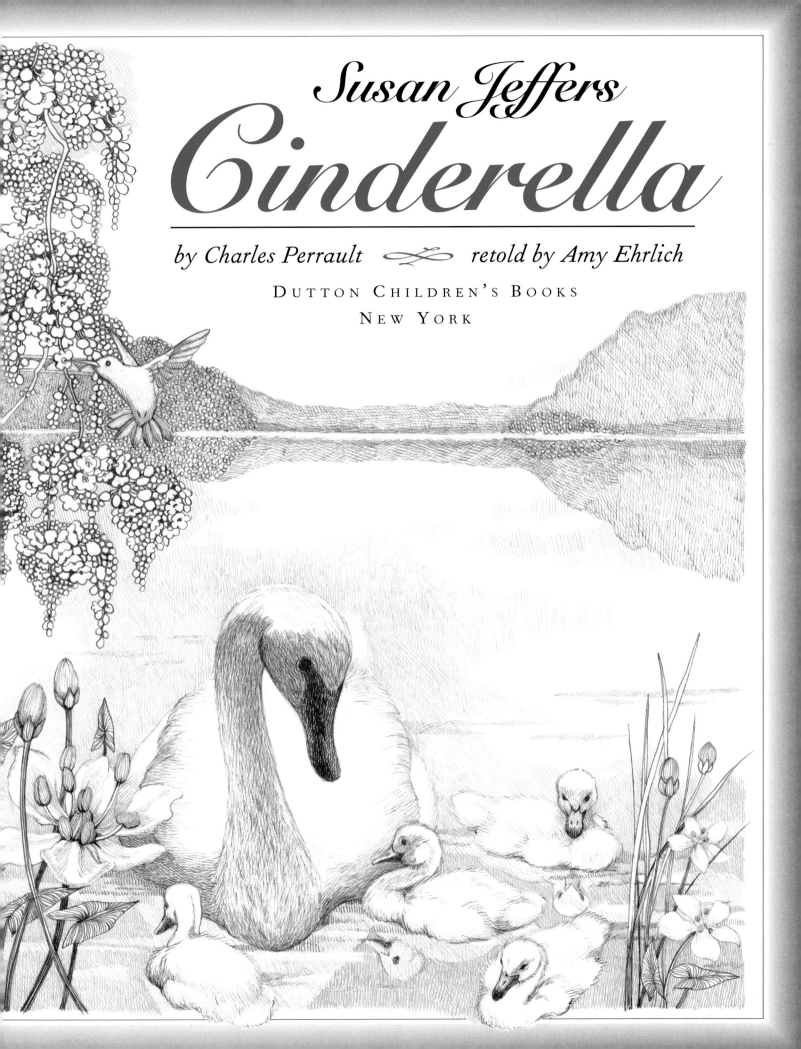

Susan Jeffers
Cinderella

by Charles Perrault   retold by Amy Ehrlich

DUTTON CHILDREN'S BOOKS
NEW YORK

Illustrations copyright © 1985, 2004 by Susan Jeffers
Text used by permission of Random House, Inc.
Text copyright © 1985 by Amy Ehrlich
All rights reserved.

Library of Congress Cataloging-in-Publication Data
Ehrlich, Amy, date.
Cinderella / text adapted by Amy Ehrlich; [illustrated by] Susan Jeffers. — 1st ed.   p. cm.
Summary: In her haste to flee the palace before the fairy godmother's
magic loses effect, Cinderella leaves behind a glass slipper.
ISBN 0-525-47345-9
[I. Fairy tales. 2. Folklore — France.]
I. Jeffers, Susan, ill. II. Cinderella. English. III. Title.
PZ8.E32Ci 2004
[E] —dc22 2004001979

Published in the United States 2004 by Dutton Children's Books,
a division of Penguin Young Readers Group
345 Hudson Street, New York, New York 10014
www.penguin.com

Originally published in 1985 by Dial Books for Young Readers, New York

Designed by Beth Herzog

Manufactured in China
1 3 5 7 9 10 8 6 4 2

The full-color artwork was prepared using a fine-line pen
with ink and dyes. They were applied over a detailed pencil drawing
that was then erased.

For the cast:
Cookie, Danielle, Karen, Patricia,
and Elizabeth

There once was a man whose wife died, and so he took another. The new wife was proud and haughty and had two daughters who were just like her in every way. But the man also had a daughter, and she was sweet and gentle and good as gold.

The wedding was hardly over before the woman began to make her stepdaughter's life a misery. From early morning until late at night the girl was forced to work, to scour the dishes and scrub the floors and pick up after her stepsisters. She did all she was asked and dared not complain to her father, who would only have scolded her, for his new wife ruled him entirely.

When she had finished her work, she used to go into the chimney corner and sit quietly among the cinders, and so she was called Cinderwench. But the younger sister, who was not quite as rude as the others, called her Cinderella. In her ragged clothing and with her dirty face, Cinderella was yet a hundred times more beautiful than her stepsisters.

After some months had passed, the king's son gave a ball and invited to it all the stylish people in the countryside. The two sisters were also invited and immediately set about choosing the gowns and petticoats, the hair ornaments and slippers they would wear. This made Cinderella's work still harder, for it was she who ironed their linen and pleated their ruffles. All day long the sisters talked of nothing but how they should be dressed.

One night, as Cinderella was helping them, they said to her, "Cinderella, would you not like to go to the ball?"

"Please, sisters, do not mock me," she said. "How could I ever dream of such a thing?"

"You are right," they answered. "People would surely laugh to see a Cinderwench at the ball."

For two days the sisters could hardly eat for excitement. So tightly did they lace themselves that they broke a dozen laces, and they were always at their looking glasses, trying on different gowns.

At last the evening of the ball came. Cinderella watched the sisters leave for the court, and when she had lost sight of them, she began to weep.

Her godmother, who was a fairy, saw her tears and asked what was the matter.

"I wish I could—I wish I could—go to the ball," stammered Cinderella, but she could say no more for crying.

"Well, then, go you shall," said her godmother. Then she told the girl to go into the garden for a pumpkin. Cinderella picked the finest she could find and carried it indoors. Her godmother scooped it out and struck it with her wand. Instantly the pumpkin turned into a fine gilded coach.

Next her godmother went to look in the mousetrap, where she found six mice, all alive. She tapped each one with her wand, and they were turned into white horses, a fine set of them to draw the coach.

But they would still need a coachman, so Cinderella brought the rat trap to her godmother. Inside there were three rats. The godmother chose the one with the longest whiskers, and as soon as she touched him with her wand, he became a fat coachman with a most imposing beard.

After that the godmother turned six lizards into footmen, who jumped up behind the coach and held on as if they had done nothing else their whole lives.

Then her godmother said to Cinderella, "Well, my dear, here is your carriage. I hope it pleases you."

"Oh yes!" the girl cried. "But am I to wear these rags to the ball?"

Her godmother simply touched Cinderella with her wand, and at once her clothes were turned into a gown of silver. Then she gave Cinderella a pair of glass slippers, the most beautiful imaginable. But as the girl was making ready to leave, her godmother warned her that she must return home by midnight. If she stayed one moment longer, her coach would be a pumpkin again, her horses mice, her coachman a rat, her footmen lizards, and her clothing would turn back into rags.

Cinderella promised she would not be late, and then she went off to the ball, her heart pounding with joy.

The king's son had been told that a great princess, unknown to all the company, would soon arrive, and he ran out to receive her himself. He gave her his hand as she sprang from the coach and led her into the hall where everyone was assembled. At once there was silence. So awed were the guests by the mysterious princess that they left off dancing, and the musicians ceased to play. Then a hushed murmur swept the room:

"Ah, how lovely she is! How lovely!"

The king's son led her across the floor, and they danced together again and again. A fine banquet was served, but the young prince only gazed at her and could not eat a bite.

After a time she left his side and went to sit by her sisters. She treated them with kindness and offered them sections of oranges that the prince had given to her. It very much pleased them to be singled out in this way.

Then Cinderella heard the clock strike quarter to twelve. Quickly she wished the company good night and ran from the hall and down the palace steps to her coach.

When she was home again, she found her godmother and thanked her and asked if she might go to the ball again the next day. As Cinderella was telling her godmother all that had happened, her two sisters came into the room.

"If you had only been there," said her sisters. "There was an unknown princess, the most beautiful ever seen in this world. She sat with us and gave us oranges."

"Was she really so very beautiful? And do you not know her name?" Then Cinderella turned to the elder one. "Ah, dear sister, won't you give me your plainest dress so that I might see the princess for myself?"

"What? Lend my clothing to a dirty Cinderwench? I should be out of my mind!" cried the sister.

Cinderella had expected such an answer, and she was very glad of the refusal. The next evening the two sisters went to the ball and she went too, dressed even more exquisitely than the first time. The king's son was always with her and spoke to her with words of praise. So entranced was Cinderella that she forgot her godmother's warning and heard the chimes of midnight striking when she thought it could be no more than eleven o'clock.

At once she arose and fled, nimble as a deer. Though the prince rushed after her, he could not catch her. In her haste, she left behind one of the glass slippers, which he picked up and carried with him.

Cinderella's coach had vanished, and she had to run home in the dark. Of her finery nothing remained but the other glass slipper. The guards at the palace gates were asked if they had seen a princess, but they replied that no one had come there but a poor country girl dressed in rags.

When the two sisters returned from the ball, Cinderella asked whether the unknown princess had again appeared. They told her yes but said she had hurried away the moment the clock struck midnight. And now the king's son had only the glass slipper she had left behind. They said he was brokenhearted and would do anything to find her once more.

All this was true. A few days afterward, the king's son proclaimed that he would marry the woman for whom the glass slipper had been made. The courtiers began by trying the slipper on all the princesses. They tried it on the duchesses and then on the ladies of the court. But nowhere in the land could they find a woman whose foot was small enough to fit the slipper. At last it was brought to the two sisters.

They pushed and pushed, trying to squeeze their feet inside, but they were not able to manage it.

Cinderella was in the room and recognized her slipper at once. "Let me see if it will fit my foot," she said.

Her sisters began to laugh and tease her. But the courtier who'd been sent with the slipper looked at Cinderella and saw that she was lovely. He said his orders were that every woman in the land must try it on.

Cinderella sat down, and he held the slipper up to her little foot. It went on at once, as easily as if it had been made of wax.

Then, while the two sisters watched, Cinderella drew from her pocket the other glass slipper and put it on too. Suddenly her godmother was there, and she touched the girl's ragged clothes with her wand, and they became a gown even more beautiful than the ones she had worn to the ball.

And now her two sisters knew she had been the unknown princess they had so admired. They threw themselves at her feet to beg her forgiveness for all their ill treatment. Cinderella bid them rise and said that she forgave them with all her heart.

Then Cinderella was taken before the prince. He was overwhelmed with love for her, and sometime later they were married. Cinderella, who was as good as she was beautiful, gave her two sisters a home in the palace, and that very same day they were married to two lords of the court.